EASY CLASSICS
EPIC COLLECTION

Published by Sweet Cherry Publishing Limited
Unit 36, Vulcan House,
Vulcan Road,
Leicester, LE5 3EF
United Kingdom

First published in the UK in 2021
2021 edition

2 4 6 8 10 9 7 5 3 1

ISBN: 978-1-78226-790-4

The Easy Classics Epic Collection: A Hero of Our Time

Cover design by Helen Panayi and Dominika Plocka
Illustrations by Helen Panayi

Lexile® code numerical measure L = Lexile® 690L

www.sweetcherrypublishing.com

Printed and bound in Turkey
T.IO006

A HERO OF OUR TIME

Mikhail Lermontov

Sweet Cherry

STORY ONE

Maxim Maximych

The traveller

Pechorin

STORY TWO

STORY THREE

Bela

Pechorin's servant

The corporal

Young man

Young woman

Young man
and woman's
grandmother

STORY FOUR

Grushnitsky

Princess Mary

Princess Ligovskoy

Vera

STORY FIVE

Vulich

Yefimich

STORY ONE:
BELA

Maxim Maximych walked wearily along the mountain footpath. The old man pulled a small cart containing everything he owned behind him. His thick, woollen coat was the same one he had worn during his time in the army, many years ago. Since then, he had been to many different places. But it was here, in the snowy Caucus mountains, that he had returned.

Maximych spotted a welcoming

boulder on the path ahead, and decided to rest. He needed to get to the next village, but it was still a day's walk away and his old army boots were rubbing his aching feet.

Maximych sighed contentedly as he rested his weary body on the boulder. He opened his steel water flask, but as he placed it to his lips, he realised there was nothing left inside.

'Would you like a drink, sir?' Maximych jumped a little and turned to see a well-dressed traveller on horseback, stretching down to hand him a shiny new flask.

Maximych nodded to the man and gratefully took the bottle. 'Where are you headed?'

When Maximych had sipped enough water to quench his thirst – but not too much so as to be impolite – he replied: 'Just to the inn in the next village.'

'You look tired, sir,' said the traveller. 'If you wish, you can hitch your cart to my horse and travel along with me. I also need to stop somewhere for the night. You could show me the way to the inn you mentioned.'

Maximych thought for a moment.

'I'm afraid I cannot pay you for the journey,' he said.

The traveller smiled. 'There is no charge,' he said kindly. 'Perhaps you could tell me a story from your time in the army?' The traveller gestured towards the shining medals that hung on Maximych's coat.

Maximych agreed gratefully, and strapped his wagon to the horse. A story was a small price to pay to save him a half day of walking.

Luckily, Maxymich had plenty of stories.

'So, what story will you tell me?' the traveller called out cheerfully, as Maximych clambered onto the cart.

Maxymich stared at the mountains as they slowly glided past and thought back to the time he was stationed in a fort nearby. One of the officers at the fort was a man called Pechorin …

'Pechorin and I often patrolled the local area together. Pechorin was

a young officer, and seemed to make friends wherever he went. He was very friendly and handsome, tall and dark. I only just came up to his shoulders!

'Pechorin was friendly with some of the local villagers. He was invited to a wedding in the village and he took me along, too.

'We sat for most of the evening with the chief of the village, his daughter Bela and his son Azamat. Although Bela was friendly and welcoming, Azamat treated her very badly. He rudely ordered her to fetch him food. We noticed that most of Bela's family treated her like a servant.

'At one point in the evening, Pechorin and Bela were deep in friendly conversation when I noticed that Azamat was missing. Soon, we heard his voice rising above the celebrations. He was arguing with a large man. The argument looked as though it may turn into a fight, so Pechorin stepped in and tried to calm the two men down. After a while it seemed as though the argument was never going to end, so we thought it was best that we left.

'On the way back to the fort, I noticed that Pechorin's face had turned serious. "What is the matter?" I asked.

"'I am worried about the chief's daughter, Bela," he replied. "Her brother, Azamat, is not a nice man." I had to agree, from what I had seen at the wedding. Pechorin continued: "Azamat was arguing over a horse. It seems that the larger man, Kazabich is his name, has the best horse in the village. Azamat would do anything to have it."

"'I see. Azamat wants to buy the horse off Kazabich, but he won't sell it to him," I said. Pechorin nodded. "That explains the argument."

'Pechorin glanced back in the direction of the village with a far off look in his eyes. "It isn't just that," he said, calmly. "Azamat promised Kazabich that if he let him buy the horse, Azamat would force Bela to work for Kazabich as his maid. Kazabich still refused."

'"Poor Bela," I said, shaking my head. "What a horrible brother to have!"

'I did not hear Pechorin mention Bela or the villagers for a few days after the wedding. But then, one morning, Pechorin came to me and asked for a favour.

"'Kazabich is on his way to the fort," Pechorin said. He was dressed in peasant clothes, rather than his usual smart army uniform.

"'Kazabich?" I asked, surprised.

'Pechorin nodded, hurriedly. It was clear he was in a rush to be somewhere. "Kazabich thinks he is coming here to sell his oats to the fort. I need you to keep him talking for as long as you can."

'I was surprised and confused at the request. "Why?"

'Pechorin grinned. "Because I am going to steal his horse!" I gasped. The peasant clothes must be a disguise!

'Before I had a chance to argue with him, Pechorin was gone. I watched his figure leave the fort and disappear into the woods. It was not long before Kazabich himself turned up at the fort, asking for me. At first, I didn't know what to say to him. It wasn't my job to buy supplies for the camp. But I had to pretend. The longer I talked to Kazabich about his oats, the more time Pechorin had to carry out his plan. As an army officer I didn't approve of Pechorin stealing a horse, but he was my friend. I didn't want this giant of a man, Kazabich, to catch him.

'After what felt like many hours, I spotted Pechorin sneaking back into the fort. He didn't have a horse with him. Instead, he was accompanied by Bela. Once I saw that my friend was safe, I made a promise to Kazabich to speak to my superiors about his oats and he left quite happily.

'Afterwards, I spotted Pechorin striding across the courtyard, dressed once again in his uniform. He looked pleased with himself.

'"What happened?" I asked, looking wide-eyed at my friend. "Did you get the horse? What is Bela doing here?"

'Pechorin grinned. "It all went according to plan, my friend," he said.

'Pechorin began to explain. Since the wedding, he could not stop thinking of poor Bela and how badly she was treated by her family. When they had spoken, she had confessed to Pechorin that she longed to escape from her father and brother.

'Pechorin had come up with a plan. He went to see Azamat and promised he would help him to steal Kazabich's horse, if he allowed Bela to leave the village.

"'And he agreed?" I asked, amazed.

"'As I said, Azamat would do anything for that horse," replied Pechorin. "And now he has it. He doesn't care about his sister."

'I breathed out heavily, taking everything in. "Where is Bela now?" I asked.

"'I have asked the kitchen staff to look after her," Pechorin said, smiling. She will have her own room and earn her own money. She is free."

'While I was happy for Bela, I was worried about what Kazabich would do when he found out his horse was missing.

'But months passed without a word. Bela was happy in her new home. She made friends, worked hard and often spent her evenings talking with Pechorin, playing cards or reading to him.

I believe she might have been a little in love with him. And, although Pechorin wasn't one to open up about his feelings, I suspected he felt the same way about her.'

The traveller had not spoken for the whole of Maximych's story. 'What happened next?' he asked, spellbound.

Maximych sighed. 'It is a sad ending, I am afraid. Just when we thought all would be well, Kazabich returned to the fort. He knew Pechorin had helped Azamat steal his horse. He waited until Pechorin was out on a patrol and he came to take Bela. In his mind, Bela belonged to him because Azamat had his horse. There was a fight. Myself and a few of the officers tried to help, but Kazabich was strong. Bela was injured.'

'Did she die?' the traveller asked, his voice no more than a whisper.

Maximych nodded. 'Kazabich escaped. We never saw him or Azamat again. Soon after that Pechorin left the army. I haven't seen him for nearly a year.'

A moment's silence fell between them. Maximych looked at the road ahead where he saw houses and chimney smoke with the sun setting behind them. 'It looks like we are nearly there,' Maximych said.

'The journey has gone quickly,' said the traveller. 'You have certainly earnt your fare. That was truly a remarkable story.'

Maximych and the traveller shook hands as they reached the inn and parted ways.

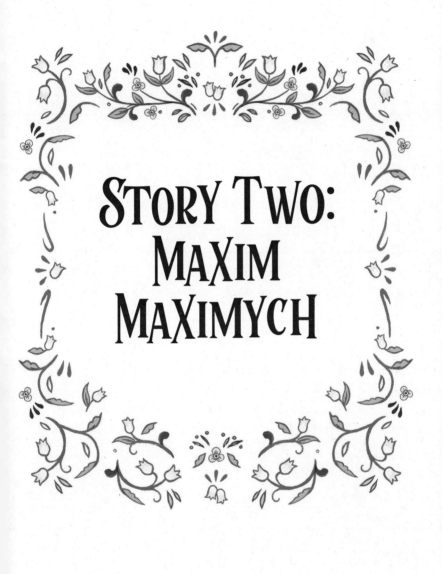

STORY TWO:
MAXIM
MAXIMYCH

Maxim Maximych stared at the innkeeper and sighed. He had just been told that if he wanted a room for the night, he would have to share.

'Very well,' Maximych said, hauling his shoulder bag across his body and following the innkeeper to the room.

As the door to the large room swung open, Maximych saw that the other occupier was the traveller who had given him a lift that very day. 'I am sorry to inconvenience you again,' Maximych said, setting his bag down on the spare bed.

The traveller looked up from the book he was reading and smiled. 'If it wasn't for you, I might not have known about the inn at all. I am happy to share the room.'

Then, a large carriage, far grander than any other carriage at the inn, pulled up outside the window. Maximych watched as a smartly dressed servant trotted out of the carriage and began to talk to the innkeeper. He handed over a bag of coins. The innkeeper nodded appreciatively to the servant and rushed back into the inn. Whoever was inside the carriage must be an important guest.

Maximych stood up and leant out of the bedroom window to get a better look inside the carriage. 'It can't be …' he said, screwing up his eyes in concentration. 'I don't believe it. It is my old friend Pechorin!'

Maximych bolted out of the room and hurried to the door of the inn just in time to see the empty carriage being taken to the stables. He looked around, frantically trying to spot Pechorin among the guests. He found only the servant from the carriage. 'Excuse me,' he said, politely.

The servant was carrying a large trunk towards the bedrooms. He sighed as he turned towards Maximych. 'Yes?' the servant said, impatiently. He looked exhausted.

'I'm sorry to bother you, but is your master called Pechorin?' Maximych asked.

'Yes, that's him,' the servant replied. 'Now if you don't mind, I must get on.' The servant began to drag the trunk along the corridor once more.

Maximych trotted after him. 'Could you tell him his old friend Maximych is here?'

The servant stopped outside a large doorway. Maximych stared at it. 'You are lucky to get a room,' he said. 'The innkeeper told us they were full.'

The servant snorted, nastily. 'There are always rooms for people who have enough money,' he said. 'Wait here.'

The servant disappeared inside the room with the trunk. Maximych could hear muffled voices coming from inside. A moment later the servant opened the door a crack and poked his face through the gap. 'My master says he will meet you outside in half an hour.'

Maximych paced up and down in front of the inn. It was dark and cold. He had been outside for over an hour, and Pechorin had not come to meet him. He glanced up to the window of the room he was sharing with the traveller. The lights were out.

As he kicked a stone along the ground, Maximych wondered how long he should wait. He knew that he and Pechorin were not considered equals. Pechorin came from a rich family, while Maximych did not. Pechorin was young and strong, while Maximych was at the end of his army service. But they had been friends during their time at the fort, and Maxymich had hoped that they still would be now.

Feeling frustrated and a little foolish, Maximych returned to his room.

The following morning, Maximych and the traveller prepared to pay their bill with the innkeeper. Just then, the traveller nudged his arm. 'Is that the gentleman you were looking for last night?' he said, gesturing towards the door where a tall, well-dressed man was standing with his servant.

Maximych smiled. 'Yes! That is him!' Maximych quickly paid his half of the room and ran to follow Pechorin onto the street.

'Pechorin!' he shouted, as Pechorin was about to step into his carriage.

Pechorin glanced round. When he saw Maximych, he slowly stepped

back down. 'Maxim Maximych,' he said, his face unsmiling. 'My servant said you were staying here.'

'He said you would meet me last night,' Maximych said. Pechorin cleared his throat awkwardly, but offered no explanation. 'Is everything all right, old friend?' Maximych asked. He suddenly wondered if he had offended Pechorin in some way, and that was why he was acting so coldly towards him. 'Do you have plans for lunch? Perhaps we could talk of old times together.'

Pechorin turned towards his carriage again. 'I'm afraid not. I am headed to Persia and I don't intend on coming this way ever again,' he said, settling himself into his seat.

Maximych stood back, confused and a little hurt. There was one last thing he needed to do before Pechorin left. 'I have something for you,' he said. Rummaging in his shoulder bag, he brought out a tattered leather journal, thick with paper. 'You left it at the fort.'

Maximych held out the journal for Pechorin to take. He had been carrying it around for months. Pechorin stared at it for a moment, then waved his hand dismissively.

'I do not want or need that anymore,' Pechorin said. As his servant climbed into the seat by the driver, Pechorin signalled for them to leave. He did not even say goodbye.

Maximych felt a wave of anger, confusion and hurt wash over him. He had believed he was friends with Pechorin, but now he knew the truth. He was rude and cold, and any friendship they had shared was over. Maximych threw the journal into the road.

'Was that the heroic Pechorin, then?' asked the traveller as he emerged from the inn. 'I have to say, he looks like a gentleman, but he doesn't act like one.'

Maximych turned round sharply, taking his anger out on his new companion. 'You are most-likely just like him. Rich enough to use people when it suits you. Give an old man a ride for a bit of entertainment!'

The traveller stood back.

'I am certainly not perfect,' he said, calmly. 'But I hope I do things out of kindness, rather than for my own gain.'

Maximych let out a long sigh. He knew the traveller had done nothing wrong. 'I am sorry, sir,' he said. 'That was not fair of me.'

The traveller smiled and buttoned up his cloak. 'Do not let it worry you. I doubt we shall meet again, so let us part as friends.' The traveller turned towards the stables to fetch his horse.

Maxymich stared at the journal lying in the road, and suddenly swooped down to pick it up. 'Perhaps you would like this for your journey,' he said, brushing the dirt off the journal and handing it to the traveller. 'It is Pechorin's diary. It is full of stories just as wonderous as the one I told you on our journey here.'

The traveller hesitated. It didn't seem right to read another man's diary. But Pechorin didn't seem to care what happened to it. The traveller took the diary with a nod of thanks. 'I am grateful to you, Maximych,' he said. 'Good luck.'

STORY THREE:
TAMAN

The traveller had been given a great gift by Maxim Maximych. The stories inside Pechorin's journal were thrilling. They kept him company as he travelled, and he shared them with friends and family for years to come.

One day, many years after he had been given the journal, the traveller read in a newspaper that Pechorin had died. He felt a strange sort of loss. He had never met Pechorin properly, but after reading his journal, he felt as though he knew him.

Soon, the traveller had an idea. He would publish the stories in Pechorin's journal so that as many

 people as possible could read them. He hoped that they would enjoy them as much as he had.

8th March 1838

After travelling for hours, we have
finally made it to the small town
of Taman. I am due to report to my
new posting in a few days' time.
The army sent me a corporal to
guide me to my new post, but he is
not very helpful. The silly boy didn't
know that there are no hotels or
inns in Taman. I must confess, I
got angry at him. I was tired and
hungry and we had nowhere to tie
up the horses.

Thankfully, a young man overheard
our conversation. I guess he is only
about fifteen years old. He has

offered us his grandma's fishing hut for the night.

As I write this, I can hear a storm approaching. I am afraid this hut is so old and fragile that one big wave will wash us out to sea. The corporal does not seem to mind. He fell asleep as soon as he lay down. But something is niggling at me. Something does not feel quite right, here.

9th March 1838

My instincts were correct. As I lay awake last night, I heard footsteps and saw a shadow cross the small window of the hut. I jumped up to see who it was and saw the young man making his way down to the shore. He looked on edge, his head twisting this way and that to see if he was being followed.

I crept out of the hut to see where he was going. After following him along the beach for about five minutes, the young man met up with a woman, only a few years older than himself. They were in deep conversation. 'Where is Yanko?' I heard the young man whisper.

'He will be here,' the young woman replied. 'He hasn't let us down before.'

After a while, a small boat appeared on the horizon, rocking

dangerously on the waves. As it got close to the shore, an older man jumped out and dragged it onto the beach. The three figures whispered in a huddle. Soon, they were taking boxes out of the boat and piling them on the beach. Whatever the

man had brought was heavy. It was clear that they did not want anyone to see what they were doing. They must be smugglers!

These people were bringing things to Taman to sell that had clearly been taken illegally from somewhere else. I should have arrested them all at that moment, but it was dark, and I was unarmed and outnumbered. Quietly, I crept back to the hut.

As the corporal and I got ready to leave this morning, the owner of the fishing hut arrived with her grandson. She was a small, elderly lady. Her hair was steel grey and her face was stern. 'Did you sleep well?' she asked.

'My companion did,' I said. 'But I am afraid I was disturbed by something that happened on the beach.' I glanced at the young man who stood up straight. A pink blush crept up his neck. 'I'm sorry to say it, but I suspect your grandson is involved in smuggling.'

The old lady seemed to grow two feet as she straightened her back. She looked me in the eye. 'I beg your pardon?' she asked, but she didn't wait for me to repeat my statement. 'I give you a place to stay for the night and you accuse my family of smuggling!'

The young man was now staring at the floor.

'I cannot deny what I saw,' I continued steadily. 'He met a young woman and a man named Yanko on the beach in the early hours of this morning. They unloaded heavy items off his boat.'

The old woman stared at her grandson. 'What were you and your sister doing with Yanko again?' she asked, accusingly. It was clear this wasn't the first time the young man and his sister had been caught with the smuggler. The young man did not answer his grandmother. She sighed and threw her hands in the air. 'Whatever you saw cannot be proved, Officer,' she said dismissively. 'And now I think it is time for you to leave.'

I couldn't help but be impressed by the old lady. She knew that her grandson had been up to something suspicious, but she was not about to let him get into trouble. I nodded and picked up my bag. 'Thank you for your hospitality,' I replied. 'Perhaps you could recommend a café where my corporal and I can eat breakfast?' I wanted them both to know that we wouldn't be leaving just yet. If I could prove something illegal had happened last night, I would.

The corporal was just as good at eating as he was at sleeping. In a small café in the centre of town he devoured his breakfast. Then, the young woman from the beach walked in, smiling and greeting the people she knew. I jumped up from my seat as the woman approached the counter. 'Can I help you, Officer?' she said, looking from my face to my uniform and back again.

'You can,' I replied. 'You can tell me what you were doing at the beach this morning with you brother and a man called Yanko.'

The colour drained from her face, but she did not let her smile drop.

'I can explain everything,' the woman said

sweetly, a nervous laugh in her voice. 'Come with me to the beach and I can show you.'

I glanced back to my corporal and decided not to take him with me. So far on our trip he had not proved to be a helpful companion. I told him to meet me in the centre of town in an hour with the horses, ready to leave. Then I followed the woman out of the café.

She didn't speak as our feet sank into the soft sand of the beach.

She headed towards a small rowing boat. 'Where are we going?' I asked. The beach was empty, and there was no sign of Yanko or the smuggled items they had hidden that night.

'I can show you better from the water,' she said, climbing in and making space for me to sit beside her. 'I'll show you where we have hidden everything.'

I climbed into the boat. We said nothing to each other as she steadily rode out into the waves. When we were a good distance out to sea, the girl pointed to a small cluster of rocks. 'There. That's where we hide everything. There's fancy food and jewels and all sorts,' she said.

As I leant a little over the side of the boat to get a better look, I felt the girl's hands on my back. She was trying to push me overboard!

She was strong, but not stronger than an officer of the Russian army. I managed to grasp her hands and push her away from me, but the struggle had made the boat rock from side to side. Water was sploshing in on both sides and the more we struggled,

the more the boat thrashed. In a flash, we had turned over.

With the heaviness of my uniform pulling me down, I pumped my arms and legs as hard as I could. I concentrated hard on getting to the surface and then aimed for the shore. I couldn't see the young woman anywhere.

As I scrambled onto the beach, my lungs felt as though they might explode from the effort of the swim. I breathed heavily, coughing up the salty water and scanning the sea for any sign of the woman. It was then that I spotted her, climbing on to the cluster of rocks she had pointed out. Relief washed over me. The young woman might have been doing wrong, but I was pleased she was safe.

Wet and exhausted, I lay on my back and stared at the sky. Should I carry on pursuing these small-town criminals? We were only in Taman on the way to a posting, not to capture smugglers. Perhaps I should let it go. I let out a long, resigned sigh. Finally, I got up and tried to dry my clothes under the weak sun. Feeling damp and exhausted, I headed to meet the corporal.

I needed to rest before setting off on our travels again, so the corporal and I headed back to the café.

To my surprise, the old woman and her grandson arrived a few hours later. They were looking for us. The young man's hands were firmly planted in his pockets, and he looked unhappy.

'I've brought you some things you ... erm ... left in the hut,' the young man said, handing me my pocket knife and some of my medals.

'They weren't left in the hut!' barked the old lady. 'He took them. It's the only reason he offered you my hut for the night.' She nudged the young man who looked like he wished the ground would open and swallow him up. 'I told him if we gave them back now there wouldn't be any trouble.'

I did not speak to the old lady, or her grandson. I silently took my belongings and stood up. 'I think it is time we were on our way, corporal,' I said.

'He's had his punishment anyway,' called the old lady as we made our way out of the café. 'His sister has left town with Yanko.'

I looked back at the young man. I saw tears well in his eyes as he quickly wiped them away with the back of his hand. I realised that this was because of me. The young woman must have thought I was going to arrest her, if not for the smuggling, then for trying to drown an army officer.

Although the young man had done wrong, it was I who started to feel guilty. As I climbed up onto my horse, I looked around the town. It was clear Taman was not a wealthy place. A young brother and sister making a few coins from smuggled goods was not the worst crime I had seen. If I had turned a blind eye, the young woman would not have felt she had to leave her home and family. I kicked my heels slightly and my horse gently walked on. I left Taman wishing that we had never come.

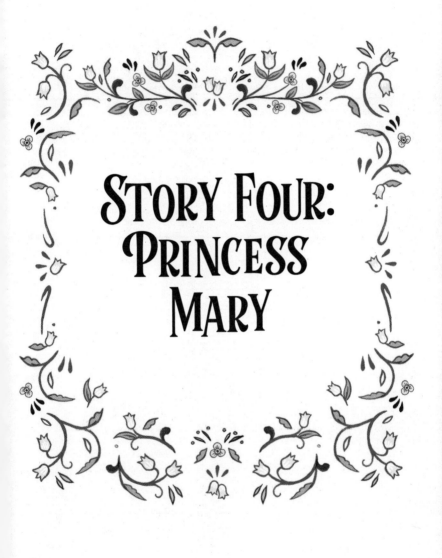

STORY FOUR:
PRINCESS
MARY

19th March 1838

We have been in Pyatigorsk for a few days now. It is one of the most pleasant places I have ever been stationed, and the perfect place to forget about everything that happened in Taman.

Pyatigorsk is well known for its natural spring water. It is said that drinking a cup of the water directly from a spring can help cure illness and keep your body healthy.

It was at one such spring that I found myself today. The Elizabeth Spring is surrounded by beautiful archways where visitors can sit in the shade and enjoy the water. It was here that I met Grushnitsky again.

Grushnitsky is a cadet, and therefore ranks far lower than me in the army. However, whenever we meet, he acts as though he is the commanding officer. He has more confidence than any man I have ever met.

'How are you, old friend?' he said, grasping my arm as though we were brothers. This annoyed me. We were not old friends. We had fought together, and I had given him orders, but we had not shared a meal or stayed up late talking and swapping stories as real friends do.

'I am quite well, cadet,' I said, reminding him that we were not equals. 'How long have you been in Pyatigorsk?'

Grushnitsky smiled. 'Long enough to get to know some of the tourists,' he said, glancing at a pair of well-dressed ladies by a fountain. 'That is Princess Mary and her mother, Princess Ligovskoy.'

I followed his gaze. The younger lady was very beautiful. She was

tall with light hair and bright blue
eyes. The older lady had the same
eyes, but her hair was a light grey.
Grushnitsky trotted over to the two
ladies to say hello.

He bowed and the ladies seemed pleased to talk to him. I found it rude of Grushnitsky not to invite me over for an introduction. It was the sort of thing a well-mannered cadet

should do for his commanding officer. But it was clear that Grushnitsky wanted to show off, and keep the princesses' attention for himself.

After a short while, the ladies left and I was forced to walk back to the army base with Grushnitsky. 'Let us walk this way,' the cadet said, taking a longer route back to our base. 'We can walk past Princess Mary's holiday house. She is staying there for three whole months!'

Soon we arrived at the gates of a grand old house. We could see the two princesses on the balcony, about to drink tea. Princess Mary smiled and waved at Grushnitsky, and did not even look in my direction. I suddenly had the horrifying thought that she may think I was the lower ranking of the two of us. It should be me who was making friends with the important people of the town! Grushnitsky glanced over his shoulder at me in triumph.

20th March 1838

Today I discovered another old acquaintance stationed in Pyatigorsk. He is a doctor named Werner and a far better friend than Grushnitsky. I was glad to see him and invited him to my quarters for tea. Werner had been in Pyatigorsk far longer than me, so I asked him how much he knew about Grushnitsky and Princess Mary.

Werner laughed. 'Now, there is a funny situation!' he said. 'Grushnitsky is in love with the princess, but he knows she will not marry a mere cadet. Somehow, he has managed to become friends with her and her mother, without revealing what rank he is. I can only assume they think he is an officer, like you.'

I was shocked. 'And what about Princess Mary?' I asked. 'How will she feel when our young friend's truth is revealed?'

Werner sighed. 'I imagine she will be rather cross!'

As we chatted, a plan started to form in my head. I was sick of Grushnitsky's behaviour. It was time someone put him straight. In fact, I was so focused on my plan, that I only caught the end of Werner's speech about Princess Mary.

'She is staying in the house for the spring, with her mother and a friend named Vera from St Petersburg.'

I sat up straight at the mention of the name Vera. Surely it couldn't be the same Vera I had known so many years ago? 'Have you met this Vera?' I asked, trying to keep my voice calm.

'What does she look like?'

Werner thought for a moment. 'She is quite pretty, I suppose. She has dark hair and green eyes. She is much shorter than the princess,' he said.

That confirmed it. It was the same Vera I had been in love with so long ago when I was a young cadet, only twenty years old. We had met at a ball in St Petersburg, and afterwards I had visited her at home whenever I

was allowed to leave my base.
Slowly, we had fallen in love. Then,
I was called to move on to another
posting. We said goodbye and lost
touch, though I have never stopped
thinking of her. To see her again
would be something marvellous. And
I am an officer now! I can show her
I have made something of myself.

21st March 1838

Today, it happened. I saw Vera again. It was both the most wonderful and most painful meeting.

But, before I write about that, I must record how I have started to put my plan of humbling Grushnitsky into action. I was at the market, enjoying the local sights and smells, when I spotted Grushnitsky, Princess Mary and her mother. Grushnitsky was being his usual self, leading the ladies through the rows of stalls, pompously explaining what each item was.

As they stopped to admire a stall selling beautifully embroidered rugs, I heard the princess say: 'Oh, the red one with the Chinese birds is wonderful! I think I shall buy it.' At that moment, I took my chance. I introduced myself to Grushnitsky in a loud voice, so that everyone's attention was on me.

I turned to the stall holder, asked him to fetch me the red rug with the Chinese birds, and bought it without a moment's thought. Then, I said goodbye to Grushnitsky and left without a single word to the princess or her mother. I noticed, with satisfaction, that the princess was frowning. She had noticed me, and she would certainly remember me the next time we met. I was already drawing her attention away from Grushnitsky.

I was still grinning as I walked back to the army base from the market. As soon as the princess became interested in me, I would innocently let her know Grushnitsky's true rank in the army. I was so pleased with myself that I almost didn't notice the figure walking towards me. It was Vera. Although it had been nearly six years

since we had met, she had not changed. She was still the most beautiful person I had ever seen. She was shocked to see me, and blushed when I said hello.

'It has been so long!' she said. 'I did not know if you were still in the army, or married ...' she stopped talking.

'I am not married,' I said, smiling. 'Are you?'

Vera nodded. I had expected that she would be married by now, but the truth still hurt my heart. 'I am staying with Princess Mary and her mother,' she said.

'So, you will be in Pyatigorsk for a few months then?' I asked, hopefully.

'Yes. We are all going to be at the military ball tomorrow evening. Will you be there?' Vera said, and I thought I saw a trace of hope in her eyes.

I nodded and a moment of silence settled between us. I wished I could fill that silence with everything I wanted to say, about how much I had missed her and how much I wished she didn't have a husband.

Instead, we said an awkward goodbye.

Tonight, my heart aches for Vera. But knowing I will see her at the ball tomorrow fills me with joy.

21st March 1838

It is late, but I could not go to sleep without recording this evening's events.

Each month, the army holds a ball for all the local aristocracy, and those visiting to drink the water of Pyatigorsk. It is always a glittering event, with a ballroom bursting with dancing couples and tables piled with food.

I wasted no time asking Vera to dance. She had been in my thoughts all day. Although she was married, her husband was not staying with her, and there was nothing improper about asking her to dance, as we were old friends.

As I held her in my arms, the years melted away. It soon felt as though no time had passed between us. As we danced, Vera quietly said: 'I have missed you so much, Pechorin.' She rested her head on my shoulder.

I was so swept up in Vera that I forgot why I had originally attended the ball. Luckily, an opportunity soon arose. Grushnitsky had not left Princess Mary's side all evening, and scowled and batted away any other man who asked the princess to dance. Finally, he broke away from her side to fetch her a drink.

'You are very attentive to the princess,' I said, joining him at the table.

'She can't do without me, Pechorin,' Grushnitsky boasted. 'I am quite her favourite officer.'

I laughed. 'But you are not an officer, Grushnitsky. You are a cadet with no promotion in sight.'

Grushnitsky reddened. 'That is not true,' he said. 'I could be promoted to officer tomorrow. In fact, they would have to promote me if I married a princess.'

I stared at Grushnitsky as he reached into his pocket and pulled out a ring. I could not help but laugh again. 'You are going to ask Princess Mary to marry you? Are you mad? She will never say yes to a cadet!'

Grushnitsky's face turned red with anger. 'We'll see,' he said as he shoved the ring back into his pocket and hurried back to the princess with drinks in hand.

Then, I overhead a group of young

women talking. They were admiring the princess, but soon the conversation turned sour.

'She thinks she is the prettiest here,' said one.

'And the best dressed,' said another, nastily.

'Well, we'll just have to do something about that,' said another, laughing viciously.

I watched as the young women stood behind the princess and waited until she had taken her drink of red fruit punch from Grushnitsky. Then, they bumped into her on purpose, making her spill the drink down her pale dress.

I had to intervene. 'Excuse me Princess, I know we have not been properly introduced, but I must speak,' I said. The princess and her mother looked at me, shocked. 'I heard these young women planning to upset Princess Mary. I believe they are jealous of her beauty.'

Princess Mary looked wide-eyed from me to the young women. 'Is this true?' demanded Princess Ligovskoy, Princess Mary's mother. The young women stayed silent, but looked ashamed of themselves.

Princess Ligovskoy was so thankful for my help that she has invited me for tea.

24th March 1838

The past few days have gone by in a blur. The morning after the ball I sent a message to Vera to meet me at the Elizabeth Fountain. We walked and talked as though it were old times. I did not want to leave our private walk. However, I had another engagement to attend.

As promised, I went for tea at Princess Ligovskoy and Princess Mary's home. I pretended to be interested in everything Princess Mary had to say, but it was Vera who I wanted to spend time with.

Princess Mary asked me about my family, my time in the army and my friends. By the end of the visit there  was not much she did not know about me. I had wanted to grab her attention away from Grushnitsky, and I had succeeded. But now that Vera was here, I wanted to finish my plan and focus all my attention on her. I decided to do what I had come here to do

'Have you seen much of our friend Grushnitsky since the ball?' I asked.

Princess Mary smiled, shyly. 'No, but I am sure he will call soon,' she said.

'He is a very nice young man,' said Princess Ligovskoy. 'I think he will ask Mary to marry him, if he can be spared from his officer's duties.'

I finally had my chance to expose Grushnitsky and I took it. 'Officer's duties?' I said, innocently. 'But Grushnitsky is just a cadet. In fact, I and the other officers have no plans to promote him to officer at all.'

Princess Mary and her mother looked shocked. I didn't stay to hear

them discuss Grushnitsky's lies. Instead, I excused myself and Vera showed me to the door. Before we said goodbye, Vera whispered to me that she was going to write to her husband to tell him she no does not love him. She knew as soon as we met again that she still felt as much love for me as I do for her. I could not be happier!

I have been challenged to a duel tomorrow morning.

When Grushnitsky discovered it was I who told Princess Mary and her mother about his lies, he was furious with me. He accused me of wanting to marry Princess Mary myself. I tried to tell him that I wasn't interested in Princess Mary, but he would not listen. Grushnitsky demanded a duel and, as a man of honour, it is impossible for me to do anything but accept. I know that duels are illegal, and especially wrong for an army officer to partake in, but I would lose the respect of the other cadets and corporals if I refused.

This evening, I asked Werner to be my second – the person who is there with me should anything bad happen. I am glad I did, as Werner overheard Grushnitsky and his friend planning to give me a gun with no bullets!

30th March 1838

My time in Pyatigorsk is over. My thoughts of a future with Vera are over too. As painful as it is to remember, I must write down what happened.

Werner and I arrived at the place Grushnitsky had set for our duel.

Before we began, I told him I knew of his plan to give me an empty gun. I saw his face turn pale as I opened the gun and filled it with bullets.

It was all over in a flash. Grushnitsky is not experienced with a gun. There was no way he could beat me. I aimed my gun at his leg so that it would only injure him. Although it was Grushnitsky who challenged me to a duel, I did not want him to die for being young and foolish.

When I returned to the army base there was a letter waiting for me from

107

Vera. Somehow her husband had discovered her plan to leave him and marry me. She was leaving with him for St Petersburg. Panic spread through me. I mounted my horse and desperately rode to Princess Mary's house. Vera had already left.

I was devastated. I had lost my true love and injured a foolish young man all in one day. However, my worries were still not over. When I returned to the base, Werner was waiting for me. He told me Grushnitsky's friend had

informed my commanding officer about the duel.

I am being transferred to a remote fort in the Caucus mountains.

STORY FIVE:
THE FATALIST

23rd July 1838

This has been one of the strangest nights I have had so far in the mountains. In a small village, not far from the fort, I have made a few friends. They like playing cards, and I enjoy getting away from the same old faces at the fort.

The evening started in the same way as many others. We played cards and talked. Then, one of the men brought up the topic of predestination — the belief that everything that happens in our lives is set out for us no matter what we do. Personally, I do not believe in it. But Vulich, one of the villagers, believes in it enthusiastically.

I put twenty gold coins on the table, which is a huge amount of money to a villager. I told Vulich that if he could prove that predestination was real, he could keep the money.

Vulich stroked his long moustache and stared at the coins. 'You have a deal,' he said, with a small smile. 'I do not believe that it is my time to die tonight. To prove it, I will shoot this gun at myself. If I do not die, then predestination is true.'

The other villagers looked at each other with concern. But they needn't have been worried. As Vulich pulled the trigger, no shot was fired. I laughed at Vulich. 'That proves nothing!' I said. 'There are no bullets in that gun, and you must have known it.'

Vulich grinned and aimed the gun at the wall. An ear-splitting shot sounded, and a hole appeared in the wall. I was stunned. There had been bullets in the gun all along.

I was astounded! Perhaps it had not been his time to die, after all. I gladly gave him the twenty gold coins, shook his hand with a smile and left the villagers to their evening.

Many hours later, I was woken by my friend and fellow officer Maxim Maximych. An incident had happened in the village and they needed officers from the fort to help out. I rushed into my uniform and followed my army major to the village.

I found the group of men I had played cards with earlier that evening. They looked serious and their faces were stained with tears. 'What has happened?' I asked, looking around the group. 'Where is Vulich?'

Vulich had been killed by a man called Yefimich. No one knew why, and Yefimich had now locked himself in his small cottage and was refusing to come out.

I struggled to take the information in. It was upsetting that a friend of mine had been killed so suddenly, but I was also shocked. Vulich had been so certain that this was not his night to die.

Groups of villagers had started to gather around the old cottage. I could see Yefimich pacing around inside. 'What is our plan?' I asked the major.

'We cannot send anyone into the cottage,' the major said, glancing round at the crowd that was growing. 'We think he may have a gun, and we can't risk anyone else getting hurt.'

But Yefimich was a murderer. He had killed an innocent man — my friend. I could feel anger

rising up inside me. I decided
that if the major would not do
anything, I would.

I waited until the major was busy
talking to the village chief, and then
I ran to the back of the cottage to
climb through a window.

My heart was beating as I awkwardly scrambled through the kitchen window. Yefimich was too concerned with what was happening at the front of his house to notice me.

When I was close enough, I jumped on him, knocking him to the ground.

He was tall and skinny, and not very strong. He fired his gun, and I felt the bullet whoosh past my ear and hit the wall behind us. It didn't take me long to knock the gun out of his hand and drag him to his feet.

We struggled out of the front door of the cottage where my fellow officers helped to tie the man's hands together.

My major immediately scolded me for disobeying his orders, but I know that he was relieved that the situation was over. The villagers slowly went back to their homes after the disturbing event, and Yefimich was taken to the nearest jail.

The adrenaline that had been coursing through me was wearing off as I reached the fort. I slumped onto my bed feeling deflated. Vulich had been a good man.

I was contemplating our last conversation about predestination when Maximych knocked on my door. 'I wanted to see how you were,' he said, stepping into my quarters. 'I understand you knew the man who was killed.'

It was kind of Maximych to be concerned about me. He is a good man. I think I will take him to the wedding I have been invited to in the village next month.

Maximych and I chatted for a while and I asked him about his thoughts on predestination. But Maximych did not understand.

Perhaps I ask too much of the people. I ask them to be who I think they should be, rather than who they really are. I was angry at the dishonesty of the young people in Taman, when all they wanted was to have a better life. Now their family is broken. I thought Grushnitsky's plans were wrong, and so I intervened. I ended up injuring him.

Now, I am alone. Vera, the one person I truly loved, was taken from me. I shall never see her again.

Once my time in the army is over, I believe the best thing I can do for myself and others is travel alone.

Then it is only I who will be affected by my actions. Only I who will suffer the consequences. For now, though, I will keep trying to be as honourable an officer as I can.

Pierre is nothing like his confident, handsome friend Andrei. He is awkward and shy – and when his father dies and leaves Pierre a vast fortune, suddenly very popular. As war rages on the edges of Moscow and the charming young Natasha catches the eye of both friends, Pierre must decide what he wants and who he is.

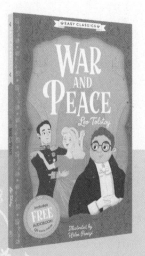

Can Pierre finally find happiness, and will Natasha decide where her heart truly lies?